W9-BMQ-268

Crazy Family Fun World is in Australia.
But it could be anywhere. . . . Yay!

Yay!

Written by Emily Rodda
Illustrated by Craig Smith

Greenwillow Books  New York

We're going to Crazy Family Fun World. Yay!

I feel car sick. Oh.

So I get to sit in front. Yay!

Then Jason gets car sick.

yay!

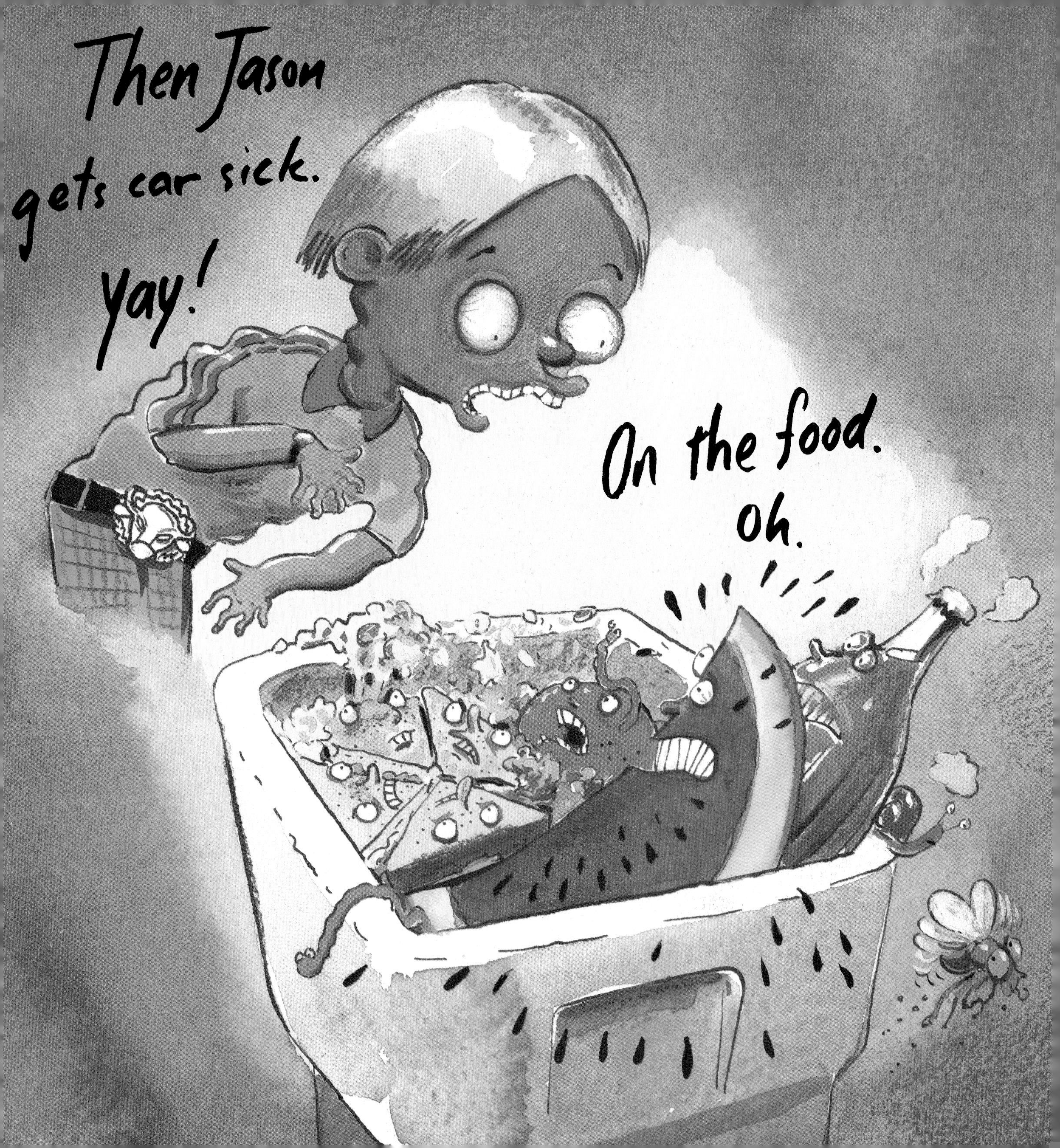

On the food.

oh.

But we can buy more food
at Crazy Family Fun World.
Yay!

The car stinks. Oh.

But then we arrive. Yay!

Uncle Todd has to rest. Oh.
So Dad takes me on
the Monster Train.
yay!

Dad freaks out. Oh.

Mum freaks out. Oh.

But I don't. Yay!

Mum has to rest. Oh.
So I take Jason into
the Mirror Maze. Yay!

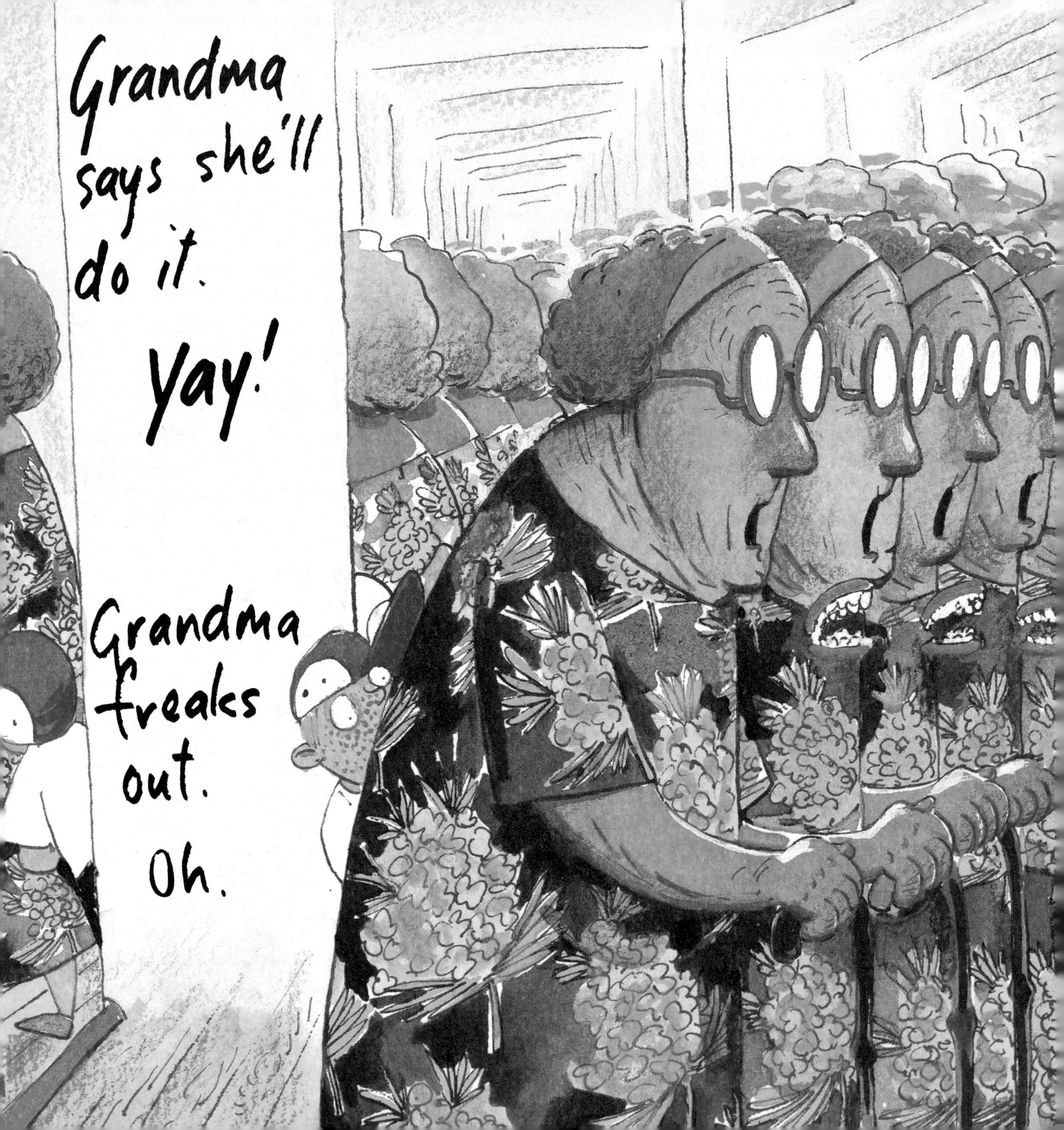
Grandma says she'll do it.
yay!
Grandma freaks out.
Oh.

The others go in after her.

Yay!

Now there's no one left to take me on the rides.

Oh.

So I go on the Wild Cow alone. Yay!

And the Bone Crusher. Yay!

THE BONE CRUSHER
NO HOT FOOD

I'm hungry. But I don't have any money. And everyone's lost in the Mirror Maze.

Oh.

So I go in and get them.

Yay!

They all have to rest.

Oh.

But they give me the lunch money.

Yay!

No one else wants any.   Oh.

So I get to eat it all myself. Yay!

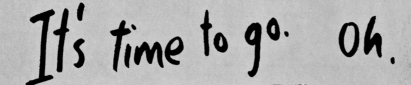

It's time to go.   Oh.

But Dad's lost the car keys.   Yay!

So while he finds them I get to go on the rides all over again.

Yay!

This day has been the BEST!

For Sue Williams
E.R.

For Daniel
C.S.

The text was hand-lettered by Craig Smith.

Text copyright © 1996 by Emily Rodda
Illustrations copyright © 1996 by Craig Smith

First published in Australia in 1996 by Omnibus Books,
part of the Scholastic Australia Group.
First published in the United States in 1997 by Greenwillow Books.

Printed in the United States of America
First American Edition 10 9 8 7 6 5 4 3 2 1

Library of Congress Cataloging-in-Publication Data
Rodda, Emily.
Yay! / by Emily Rodda ; pictures by Craig Smith.
— 1st American ed.
p.   cm.
Summary: Jason and his family have a full
day when they go to Crazy Family Fun World.
ISBN 0-688-15255-4
[1. Amusement parks—Fiction.]
I. Smith, Craig, (date) ill.
II. Title.   PZ7.R5996Yay
1997   [E]—dc21   96-46251   CIP   AC